MILE END

To urban kids around the world who illuminate
concrete alleys with their brimming imaginations,
starting with Arnaud and Florent, my own
two Mile Enders and inspiration.

Special thanks to my friend and agent, Kirsten Hall, whose sense
of wonder and intuition guided me toward this adventure.

Text and illustrations copyright © 2017 by Isabelle Arsenault

Tundra Books, a division of Random House of Canada Limited,
a Penguin Random House Company

Library and Archives Canada Cataloguing in Publication
Arsenault, Isabelle, 1978–, author
      Colette's lost pet / Isabelle Arsenault.
Issued in print and electronic formats.
ISBN 978-1-101-91759-6 (hardback). —ISBN 978-1-101-91761-9 (epub).
     I. Title.
PS8601.R7538C64 2016   jC813'.6   C2016-902180-7   C2016-902181-5

Published simultaneously in the United States of America
by Random House Books for Young Readers

Edited by Tara Walker and Maria Modugno
Designed by Isabelle Arsenault and Kelly Hill
The artwork in this book was rendered in pencils, watercolor and ink
with digital coloration in Photoshop.
Handlettering by Isabelle Arsenault.

Printed and bound in China
www.penguinrandomhouse.ca

1 2 3 4 5 6   22 21 20 19 18 17

Penguin
Random
House

TUNDRA BOOKS

A Mile End Kids Story

COLETTE'S LOST PET

Words and pictures by
ISABELLE ARSENAULT

TUNDRA BOOKS

Hey, Lily!

Have you seen Colette's lost pet? It's a parakeet.

Gee, that's not the kind of bird I usually see around here. What color is it?
Um, well . . .
uhhh . . . It's blue!
With a bit of yellow on its neck.

What does it
sound like?

Um, well . . . uh . . .

Like PRrrrrrr
Prrrr PrrrrruiiiiiiT!

And it speaks a
little bit, too.

But only
in French.

Bien sûr!

Aw, cute!
I haven't heard it
but I did hear
Beth's cat meowing.
It passed by just
a minute ago . . . .

Oh!

To Beth's!

Don't worry, Colette.
We'll find Marie-Annette!

Marie-Antoinette!

Hey, Beth!

Have you seen Colette's lost pet? It's a parakeet. It's blue with a bit of yellow on its neck, its name is Marie-Antoinette and it makes a sound like PRrrrrr Prrrr PrrrrruiiiiiiT!

I don't think so.
Do you have a picture
of it?

Um, well . . .

uh . . .

Too bad I don't
have that great shot
we took in . . .

uh, Hawaii.

I can draw it
though!

Let me see.
Is this your bird's
actual size?

Um, well . . . uh . . .

yes, pretty much,
I guess.

But . . .

It's gained some weight lately . . . .
It kind of grew bigger
and bigger.
So I had to get a bigger cage
and then a bigger house.

Until it became <u>TOO BIG</u>
to fit in the house!

But then it was the perfect
size to fly around!

So we traveled
the world.

I'm telling you,
this parakeet is <u>truly</u>
amazing!

It's just the best
pet you could ever
dream of . . .

and it's MINE!

Colette!

CLARK ALLEY